Focus

The focus of this book is:

- to develop children's speaking and listening through mind mapping,
- to use a contents page to find specific information.

Tuning In

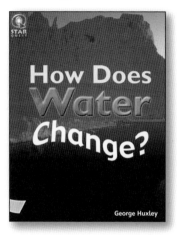

The front cover

Let's read the title together.

If you were going to answer that question (How does water change?) what would you say?

The back cover

Let's read the blurb and see if the book is going to answer the question in the same way we did.

Is this what we expected the book to be about?

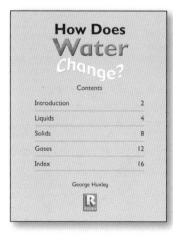

Contents

How many different forms can water have?

Let's read the list of contents together.

We are going to choose which section to read – Liquids, Solids or Gases, but first we are going to read the Introduction.

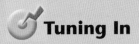
Tuning In

What were the different forms water can have?

What have you noticed about the text on these two pages?

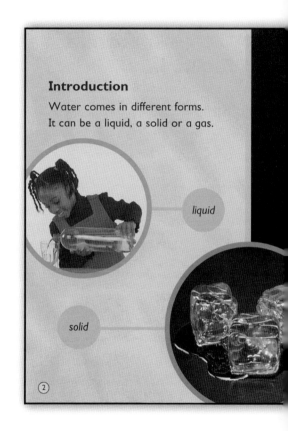

Introduction

Water comes in different forms.
It can be a liquid, a solid or a gas.

liquid

solid

gas

😊 Prompt and Praise

Check that the children have read 'liquid', 'solid' and 'gas' correctly.

Check the children have located the words next to the illustrations.

Speaking and Listening

Go back to the Contents and choose a section to read.

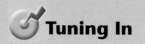 **Tuning In**

Why is the girl able to pour the water easily? (It moves freely.)

Liquids

When water is in a liquid form, it moves freely. The water in the glass is in a liquid form.

Where else can you find water in a liquid form?

 **Prompt and Praise**

Check that the children are using the punctuation.

Speaking and Listening

Where else can you find water as a liquid?

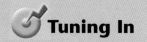

Tuning In

How does the water in a river move? (It moves freely.)

The water in a river is in a liquid form.
The water in a river moves freely.

😊 Prompt and Praise

Praise children who are reading with fluency.

🎯 Tuning In

How does water feel when it is solid?

How is water different when it is a solid? (It keeps its shape.)

What is the photograph of?

> **Solids**
>
> When water is in a solid form, it is hard. It keeps its shape.
>
> *Where else can you find water in a solid form?*

😊 Prompt and Praise

Check that the children are paying attention to the punctuation.

Speaking and Listening

Where else can you find water as a solid?

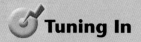

Tuning In

What is the photograph of?

Is an iceberg made of water?

The water in an iceberg is in a solid form. The water in an iceberg is hard.

😊 Prompt and Praise
If children find 'iceberg' difficult, break the word into two words.

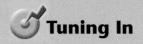 **Tuning In**

Look at the steam coming out of the kettle.

What has happened to the water inside the kettle?

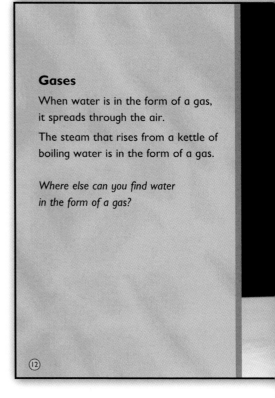

Gases

When water is in the form of a gas, it spreads through the air.

The steam that rises from a kettle of boiling water is in the form of a gas.

Where else can you find water in the form of a gas?

 Prompt and Praise

If children find 'through the air' difficult, prompt by directing them to the photograph.

Speaking and Listening

Why should you never put your hand near the steam?

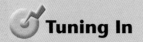
Tuning In

In some places in the world, lakes and pools are very hot from the earth underneath. We call these 'hot springs'.

What can you see in the photograph?

The steam that rises from a hot spring is water in the form of a gas.
As the steam rises, it spreads through the air.

😊 Prompt and Praise

If children find 'through the air' difficult, prompt by directing them to the photograph.

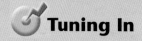 **Tuning In**

This page is called an index. What would we use it for?

Which pages would have 'liquid' in the text?

Look at page 4. How many times is 'liquid' written?

Prompt and Praise

Check that the children can locate the words in more that one place.